Was that someone moving? Or had he just seen his own reflection in a mirror? Chuckie trembled. Then he heaved a sigh of relief. It *was* just a mirror. His reflection stared back at him.

Then his reflection scratched its nose.

"AAAAAH!" shrieked Chuckie. His reflection stepped into the light.

Chuckie found himself staring at another baby. The baby looked exactly like him.

Rugrats Chapter Books

#1 The Perfect Formula

#2 Tommy's Last Stand

#3 Star-Spangled Babies

#4 Bonjour, Babies!

#5 Chuckie's Big Wish

#6 Just Wanna Have Fun

#7 Angelica the Grape

#8 Book 'Em, Tommy!

#9 It Takes Two!

#10 Dil in a Pickle

#11 Stupid Cupid

#12 Prince Chuckie

Prince Chuckie

KLASKY CSUPO INC.

Based on the TV series *Rugrats*® created by Arlene Klasky, Gabor Csupo, and Paul Germain as seen on Nickelodeon®

ISBN 0-439-35199-5

12 11 10 9 8 7 6 5 4 3 2 1   1 2 3 4 5 6/0

Printed in the U.S.A.

First Scholastic club printing, September 2001

Prince Chuckie

by Sarah Willson
illustrated by Ed Resto

SCHOLASTIC INC.

New York Toronto London Auckland Sydney
Mexico City New Delhi Hong Kong Buenos Aires

Chapter 1

"I can't believe we're actually going to meet a real king!" Didi said to the others as they entered the lobby of a fancy hotel. It was crowded with well-dressed people.

"And I can't believe he married a regular person!" marveled Chas. He was carrying Chuckie and tugging on his own bow tie. It came unclipped in his hand. "The new queen is an ordinary American woman. Apparently, they met in his country when her tourist bus had a fender bender with his royal motorcade. It was love at first sight!"

"Looks like a pretty swanky shindig," said Betty, who was carrying Phil. "The queen was born around here, so they've invited the whole town to this party."

"It was nice of them to invite kids, too," said Kira. "I hear the king has a son already, and the new queen has a daughter."

Didi smoothed the stiff collar on Dil's sailor suit and adjusted her own ruffled neckline. Then she sighed. "Imagine having a king fall in love with you, and suddenly becoming a queen!"

They could hear the sound of music playing and glasses tinkling. Two doormen opened the heavy gold doors for them and showed them into the banquet hall.

"It must be every little girl's dream to

be made a princess!" said Kira.

"What did you say, princess?" Drew was asking Angelica as the others joined them inside the crowded room.

"I said I'm ready to meet the king and queen now!" Angelica bellowed over the noise of the music. "You promised I could see a real live king and queen. I've been practicing my song and dance and curtsy for a week!"

"There, there, honeycakes," Drew said soothingly. "I'm sure you'll get a chance, but right now Mommy and Daddy are waiting our turn to shake hands with the king and queen. You never know when something like that could advance Daddy's career. Why don't you play with the other kids while we wait?" He patted her head absently.

Angelica glared at the babies, who were sitting on the floor near the punch bowl table.

Drew turned to Stu. "This is some party, eh bro? Didn't I tell you it would be fancy? Try to be on your best behavior, would you?"

"Yeah, sure," said Stu. He reached toward the tray of a passing waiter, then stared down at his hand. It was covered with black slimy stuff. "Yikes! What kind of grub are they serving in this place, anyway?"

"That's caviar," Drew said with a smirk.

Stu plunged his hand into a nearby champagne bucket. He wiped it off on his tuxedo.

"There they are!" Didi cried, pointing across the room at the king and queen, who had just entered.

"Tommy," Chuckie whispered, plucking at Tommy's sailor suit. "What is this place? And why are we wearing these itchy clothes? They're makin' the boo-boos on my elbows hurt."

"We're at a party for a king and a queen," said Tommy. "They're on their humming-moon."

"I wonder where the prince and princess are." Kimi said, peering through grown-ups' legs.

"Don't you babies know anything?" scoffed Angelica. "The prince won't be here. I heard my mommy say that he's a spoiled little brat. He probably throws people in the dumb-geon if he doesn't get his way!" She thought about this for a moment. "On the upper hand, maybe he's on to something."

Just then one of the waiters picked up a bottle of sparkling water and twisted off the top. Water sprayed all over Chuckie, soaking him. The waiter didn't seem to notice.

"I don't like this party one bit!" Chuckie spluttered, staring down at his sopping wet clothes. Water dripped from his glasses, making it hard for him to see anything. "Where's my daddy? He always has extra clothes for me to change into." He groped his way through the crowd of grown-ups.

"Chuckie, wait!" Tommy called after him. "You're going the wrong way! Your daddy's right over there!"

But Chuckie didn't hear Tommy. He felt his way through the crowd of grown-up legs. No sign of his dad. He kept walking, but couldn't see a thing. The music suddenly faded. Where was he? He took off his glasses to wipe them dry, then put them back on again.

"Uh-oh," Chuckie said out loud. He was standing in a large room. Dark and hushed, it seemed to be empty, although a television was on. "I must have got losted." Chuckie shivered, then began to tug off his wet clothes.

Was that someone moving? Or had he just seen his own reflection in a mirror? Chuckie trembled. Then he heaved a sigh of relief. It *was* just a mirror. His reflection stared back at him.

Then his reflection scratched its nose.

"AAAAAH!" shrieked Chuckie. His reflection stepped into the light.

Chuckie found himself staring at another baby. The baby looked exactly like him.

Chapter 2

"Wh-wh-who are you?" Chuckie asked in amazement.

"Who am I?" said the kid. "Who am I? How dare you address me like that! On your knees, minion!"

"Huh?" Chuckie said, staring down at his knees. "What's on my knees? Did I spill something?"

"No, I mean, kneel down!" the baby demanded impatiently. "That's what you're supposed to do when you meet a royal prince, and I'm a prince."

"Oh," said Chuckie. He sank to his knees.

"I am Prince Maximilian Rupert Walter Hornsworth the Seventh. But you can call me Your Highness."

Chuckie looked up curiously at the baby standing before him. Prince Maximilian was exactly the same size as Chuckie. He had freckles sprinkled across his nose, two baby teeth protruding from his mouth, and unruly red hair. He wore no clothes, except for a pair of training pants that were made of a shimmery golden fabric.

"Excuse me for sayin' so, Your Highliness, but I couldn't help noticing that we look just like each other!" Chuckie said. "'Ceptin the glasses."

Prince Max eyed Chuckie with interest. "Stand up," he commanded.

Chuckie scrambled to his feet. He

wasn't wearing any clothes, either, having managed to work his way out of his soaking wet outfit.

"Wow," said Prince Max. "We do look alike. Hand me your glasses."

"I can't see too good without them," Chuckie said as he hesitantly took them down from his nose.

Prince Max snatched them from his hand and put them on. "It's all blurry with these things on," he said crossly.

"It's blurry with them off," said Chuckie.

They stood side by side at the mirror.

"How come you don't have any clothes on, Your High 'n' Mightiest?" asked Chuckie.

"I won't let Perkins the butler get me dressed for this dumb old party," said Max. "He's gone to find some chocolate for me. Sometimes I let him dress me when he gives me chocolates."

"You mean you don't want to go to your daddy's party?"

"No way," said Max.

"But why not?" asked Chuckie. "Don't you like your new mommy and sister?"

"Are you kidding?" said Max. "Everybody knows stepmothers are wicked. They send kids out into the woods so they get lost, or they feed them poison apples. No way. Not for me. I'm having nothing to do with my new mommy. And I don't need a new sister, either."

"Gee," said Chuckie. "I guess I got lucky. I got a new mommy but she's really nice. And so is my new sister."

Prince Max thought this over, then his face clouded. "What do you know?" he sneered. "You're just a commoner, anyway." He turned around to glance at the television, which was still on. "The only good thing about being here in

America is this great cartoon. It's called *Blammo-Man*. I love it."

"That's the scardiest cartoon on TB!" said Chuckie. "I never watch it. But I guess bein' a prince and all, you're probably not scareded of anything, are you?"

Prince Max shook his head proudly.

"Could I have my glasses back now, please?" asked Chuckie.

"Hold on. Someone's coming," said Max. He ducked behind a curtain just as a man in a fancy butler's uniform came bursting in.

"Now, now, Your Highness!" said the man. He was holding out a huge bar of chocolate. "We'll just slip you into these clothes. There's a nice prince. No need to be naughty."

Before Chuckie knew what was happening, the butler had stooped down and picked Chuckie up. He pulled a jewel-laden shirt over Chuckie's head and thrust his arms firmly into the sleeves. Then he draped a heavy satin cape across Chuckie's shoulders and plunked a crown on his head. The butler picked Chuckie up and turned to leave the room.

Still wearing Chuckie's glasses, Max stepped out from behind the curtain and watched them, open mouthed.

No sooner had the door shut than it swung open again. Chas burst in panting. "There you are, Chuckie!" Chas said in relief. He picked up Prince Max. "I thought I'd lost you! It's time for us to go home." He noticed the soggy pile of clothing that Chuckie had taken off earlier, and picked it up. "How did these get so wet? Oh, never mind. I brought along some spares. Here we go. Everyone's waiting for us in the car!"

Prince Max was too stunned to protest as he was whisked from the room.

Chapter 3

Chuckie awoke the next morning to the sound of his bedroom door opening. "Good day, Your Majesty," said a voice he didn't recognize. "Your new mother, the queen, will be in to see you soon."

Chuckie sat up in alarm. He looked around for his teddy bear and his favorite, ratty old blankey that he always slept with. Instead he found himself clutching a satin blanket. He groped wildly for his glasses, but all he could find on the nightstand was a heavy gold crown. Then he remembered everything that had happened the night before. He began to cry softly.

"Now then, Your Highness, I am sure you don't wish to be disagreeable again today," Perkins the butler said with a tight smile. He helped Chuckie out of his long lacy white nightshirt, then dressed him in a stiff, jeweled shirt and a heavy cape. Chuckie could barely move in it. Perkins placed the crown on Chuckie's head. It felt cold and heavy and made Chuckie's head hurt. "I shall go check on Your Highness's royal breakfast," he said. With a bow, he left the room.

"I miss my daddy," Chuckie said to himself miserably. "And my blankey and my oatmeal for breakfast and all my friends." He started to sniffle. He was sniffling so loudly, he almost didn't hear the door to his room open again. In walked a little girl. She was about the same age as Angelica. Her hair was long and brown. She was dressed in a gown studded with jewels and wore a crown on her head. The crown kept slipping down over one eye.

"Well?" she said warily to Chuckie. "Aren't you gonna scream and make me leave again?"

"Why should I do that?" Chuckie asked, squinting to see her.

"Because that's what you usually do," she said. "Every time I try to talk to you, you call me a commoner and throw something at me. Are you going to do that again?"

"N-n-n-o," Chuckie stammered. "I think I better eggs-plain something here. I'm not Prince Max. I'm Chuckie, just a normal American baby. We switched places by accident and—"

She glared at Chuckie suspiciously, as

if she thought he was trying to trick her. Her brow furrowed. "If you're really a normal American baby, then answer this trip-ya question." She thought for a moment. "What great American candy bar turns your tongue green?"

"Reptar Bars," Chuckie said without hesitation.

"Wow," she said slowly. "I don't think my new brother would know the answer to that." She peered carefully at his face. Her jaw dropped. "You're tellin' the truth! You look just like him! But you really *aren't* him, are you?"

Chuckie shook his head miserably. His crown slipped over one ear.

"Well!" the girl said, brightening. "I guess that eggs-plains why you're not throwing stuff at me like he usually does." She grinned. "I'm Princess Isabel. I didn't used to be a princess until my mommy married the king. Now I have to act like a princess all the time."

"Don't you want to be a princess?" asked Chuckie.

"No way. Everyone's making me do stuff I don't like to do. I have to wear uncomforter clothes like this"—she tugged at her dress—"and they feed you weird food and you're not allowed to go to the playground or dig in the mud or really even play at all. And I have to learn boring stuff all day long. Who cares about the hissitry of the royal family? And my new brother, Prince Max, was being mean to me, which was making it all much worser. Max is a royal brat. But you seem much nicer than him. It'll be better to be your sister instead."

"Oh, no!" Chuckie said in horror. "I'm sorry, really I am, but I can't be your brother forever. I got my own sister at home, see, and I have a new mommy, and I miss my daddy. It was all a big mistake. I gotta find the real prince and switch back so I can see my daddy again."

Perkins entered the room again, staggering under the weight of a heavy gold tray laden with golden items. He plunked it down on the table, then stood up and stared curiously at Chuckie and Princess Isabel. "Well! It is delightful to see the two of you getting along!" He bowed and left the room again.

Isabel gave a disappointed sigh. "Oh, well. It's too bad you're not going to be my brother," she said. "But you better start acting like him for now. Here." She handed Chuckie a golden sippy cup. "Don't let it fall on your toe. It hurts, believe me."

Chuckie nearly dropped the heavy cup but managed to heave it onto the table in time.

"You'll get used to all this stuff," she said. "See ya later. I gotta go to my needlepointing lesson. I'm supposed to be needlepointing the Royal Goat of Arms, whatever that is." She stomped out of the room and closed the door.

Chapter 4

Tommy, Phil, and Lil were playing in the playpen. The Finster family had just arrived at Tommy's house. As soon as Chas and Kira had joined the other grown-ups in the kitchen, Kimi hurried over to the other babies.

"There's something wrong with Chuckie," she whispered to them in a worried voice. "He's walking around saying he's really a prince. And also he doesn't want to play with me. All he

wants to do is watch *Blammo-Man* on TB."

"*Blammo-Man?*" Tommy repeated in disbelief. "But that's the scarediest cartoon there is! Chuckie never watches that."

The babies all turned to look over at the baby they thought was Chuckie. He had marched right over to the TV and turned it on. Then he had turned over a plastic toy bin and climbed onto it to watch. On his head he wore a creased cardboard crown, the kind that came from a fast-food restaurant. Around his shoulders he wore a hand-towel as a cape.

"I'll go talk to him," said Tommy. He walked over to Prince Max. "Uh, Chuckie?"

Prince Max looked crossly at Tommy. His glasses were pushed way down on his nose, and he stared over the tops of them. "Like I told that other commoner baby, I am not Chuckie. I am Prince Max.

We got switched at the party."

"Um, well, Prince Max, could I look at your elbows for just a minute?"

Max looked at Tommy curiously. "You sure have strange customs in this country," he said as he bent his arms and pointed his elbows at Tommy. Then he lowered them and turned back toward the TV. "And now," he said, "I must watch this show. We don't have it in my country. You may go." He waved Tommy away with his hand.

Tommy turned around and walked back to the others.

"What did he say?" asked Kimi.

"He's telling the truth," said Tommy. "He really isn't Chuckie. Chuckie had boo-boos on his elbows. I was there when he felled down and got them. But this baby doesn't. And, anyway, the real Chuckie would never be watching *Blammo-Man*. He must be Prince Max!"

Angelica had been playing with her Cynthia doll across the room. She looked up. "Oh brother," she scoffed. "Of course it's Chuckie. He's just trying to get a ten-shun. *I'm* the one who should be treated like royalty around here!" She came over and sat down on Max's crate, which caused Max to tumble off the other side. His crown rolled off his head. Angelica reached down, picked it up, and plunked it on her own head.

"Angelica!" Tommy said, rushing over to help Max to his feet. "He really *is* a prince. You better act nice to him!"

Prince Max brushed himself off and then glared at Angelica over the tops of Chuckie's glasses. "You have hurt my royal feelings. When I get my kingdom back, I'm going to have you thrown into the dumb-geon!"

Angelica rolled her eyes. "Yeah, right. Sure, Chuckie." She turned back to the TV.

"I'm sorry about my cousin, Prince Max," said Tommy. "She sometimes has trouble being nice to us babies. Would you, um, like to play with my toys over there?" he asked.

Max crossed his arms and frowned. "No. I am a prince. Princes aren't supposed to play with toys."

"What do they do, then?" Tommy asked curiously.

"Just sit around," Max said gloomily. "You may go." And he walked over to the couch and sat down, his nose held high.

Tommy hurried back over to where the other babies were standing. "We gotta make a plan," he whispered.

"What kind of plan, Tommy?" asked Phil.

"We gotta get Chuckie back. Wherever he is, he's prob'ly feeling scared and lonely. He prob'ly misses us. We gotta figure out how to switch them back again. I wonder what Chuckie's doing right now?"

Chapter 5

Meanwhile, back at the hotel, the king and queen were just returning from a shopping trip. "Do you think Isabel and Max are getting along all right?" the queen asked nervously.

"I'm sure they are," said the king, who didn't sound sure at all.

"I hope Max warms up to us soon," she said. "Maybe I'll go see him and try again."

"Whatever you think, my dear," said

the king. "I know Max can be a difficult child at times."

The queen took a deep breath and entered Max's room.

Chuckie and Isabel were sitting quietly next to each other on a couch, turning the pages of a picture book. The queen did her best to hide her astonishment.

"Mommy!" Isabel yelled, jumping off the couch and running into her mother's arms.

"Why, aren't you two playing nicely!" she said.

"Yes, Mommy, he's a nice baby," Isabel said, smiling sweetly. "May I go see what you brought me?"

"Of course," said the queen. She watched Isabel scamper from the room. Then she came over and sat down next to Chuckie. "Max, honey, you really are a nice little boy, aren't you?" She reached out a tentative hand toward Chuckie.

Chuckie couldn't see her face very well without his glasses, but she seemed nice. He moved closer to her and tried not to think about how much he was missing his own daddy.

The king walked in just at that moment. His jaw dropped. Then he spoke. "Why, Max, how nice of you to welcome your new mother!" he said.

Chuckie smiled and snuggled closer to the queen.

The king beamed. "There, you see, my dear? I told you the two of you would get along splendidly!" He extended his arm to the queen, who took it and walked out of the room.

"Wow, she's not a wicked step-mommy at all!" Chuckie said to himself. "I gotta remember to tell Prince Max that." He sighed. "I just hope Max is being nice to *my* daddy and my friends."

Chapter 6

"I'm worried about Chuckie," Chas said in a low voice. It was two days later, and he was in the Pickleses' kitchen with Betty, Howard, Stu, and Didi. Dil was in his bouncy seat. Chas pulled aside the curtain to look out the window at the babies, who were playing in the backyard. "He's been wearing that crown and that cape ever since we were at that party for the royal family."

"I wonder what Dr. Lipschitz would

think," Didi said, pursing her lips thoughtfully as she warmed a bottle for Dil. "He would probably say that Chuckie's make-believe play is perfectly normal behavior for a child who has just experienced the introduction of a new sibling."

"Yeah, he's just in a phase," said Betty.

"Maybe he's not feeling well," said Howard.

"By the way," said Stu, who hadn't been paying attention to the conversation, "did I mention what a nice chat I had with the king at the party?"

"Yes, Stu." Didi sighed. "Many times. I believe you, even if Drew doesn't."

"You all were so busy looking for Chuckie, you didn't see us. But the king was really interested in the toys I've invented. In fact, I even gave him my card and invited him to stop over to see my workshop sometime."

"Maybe I should take Chuckie to the doctor," said Chas, who was still looking out the window.

In the backyard, Grandpa Lou lay on his lawn chair, snoozing behind his newspaper. Angelica was in the sandbox, playing with her Cynthia doll. Max sat nearby on an overturned laundry basket, watching the other babies, who had discovered a squishy mud puddle.

Max slid down from his perch and approached them cautiously. "What are you doing?" he asked them, trying to sound like he didn't care.

"We're makin' mud pies," explained Phil, who was patting a lump of mud into a flat, mucky circle.

"With worms on top," Lil said, holding up a squiggling worm for him to see.

"And Kimi and I are makin' a castle out of the mud," said Tommy.

Max squatted down next to Tommy

and Kimi. "You need someone who's an expert on castles to help you," he said. "Move over. I command you."

Tommy and Kimi looked up at Max. When they didn't move over, Max was quiet for a moment. "I mean, excuse me, could I help you make a castle?" This time he used a much nicer tone.

Tommy and Kimi smiled. "Sure, Max," Tommy replied.

Suddenly Angelica walked up and snatched the crown off of Max's head. "Sorry, *Prince* Chuckie," she said sarcastically. "I need this crown to go riding on my royal tricycle." And she dashed away.

The other babies gasped and turned toward Max. But he just shrugged. "She should learn how to be nicer," he said. Then he quietly untied the towel-cape from around his neck and threw it to one side. He sat down in the mud and picked up a pail. Phil and Lil came over and joined them. Lil took off her shoes, and Phil began to fill them up with mud. Grinning, Max took off his own shoes and began to do the same thing. "I never get to have fun like this at home," Max said ruefully. He began to sniffle a little bit. "Even so, I miss my daddy. I want to go home!"

"Don't worry, Max," said Tommy. "We'll get you home again."

"Yeah, we'll think of something," said Kimi.

Max smiled through his tears. "You are nice. When I get back to my kingdom, I'm going to make you all knightses and ladies."

"What's that?" asked Phil.

"It means everybody has to call you 'Sir Phil' and 'Lady Lil,'" said Max. Then he frowned. "But I'm going to have that Angelica thrown into the dumb-geon for being so mean."

Chas was still watching them through the window. He smiled. "Looks like Chuckie is feeling like himself again," he said to the other grown-ups.

Chapter 7

Back in the Pickleses' yard, Max was explaining to Tommy, Kimi, Phil and Lil what it was like to be a prince. "It used to get pretty lonely," he said sadly. "I used to think that because I was a prince I shouldn't play with other babies. But now I see how fun it is. I bet your friend Chuckie would rather be playing in the mud with us than whatever he's doing right now."

"Yeah, we got to think of a way to switch

you and Chuckie back," said Tommy.

"I know," said Max. "But how are we going to do that? Back when I lived like a prince, it was easy to make things happen. All I had to do was ring a little bell and everybody came running."

"Did your daddy come running too?" asked Kimi.

"Well, usually Perkins came first. But then all I had to do was throw a big tandrum and he'd go get my daddy."

"And all you did was ring a bell to get all that to happen?" asked Lil in amazement.

"Yeah. It worked every time."

Suddenly Tommy brightened. "That's it! That's the plan!"

"*What's* the plan, Tommy?" asked Phil.

"All we gots to do is find a bell so Max can ring it. Then Max's daddy will come running over here. And he'll have Chuckie with him, and he and Max can make the switch!"

"But where are we going to find a bell?" Kimi asked, looking around the yard.

Tommy thought hard. Then he jumped up. "Angelica has a bell on her tricycle!" he said. "We'll go ring that one!"

Just then the babies heard a familiar voice. "Outta my way, Drool-Machines! Make way for Princess Angelica!" Still wearing Max's paper crown, Angelica zoomed into the backyard on her tricycle. She came to a stop in front of the babies. "What are you babies starin' at?" she asked suspiciously.

"We were wondering if we could ring the bell on you tricycle," said Tommy.

Her eyes narrowed. "How come?"

"Max says if he rings a bell it will bring his daddy and Chuckie over to our house."

"Don't tell me you still believe that nonsense Chuckie's been sayin'," Angelica scoffed. Then she smiled slyly. "Okay, he can ring the bell. But under one conditioner."

"What?" said Tommy.

"I'll let him ring it once, but then you babies have to bow to me and call me 'Your High Nest' and do whatever I tell you to do."

"You are not very nice, Angelica," said Max. "I'm going to remember this when I'm a prince again."

Angelica snorted, but she sat back on her bicycle seat and crossed her arms. Max took a hesitant step toward the bike and rang the bell.

Nothing happened.

"Nice try, Chuckie," said Angelica. "My dad's taking me shoe-shopping now. You babies can start practicing your bowing for when I get back." She flounced back into the house.

"Gee, I'm sorry," Max said, hanging his

head. "It used to work when I was a prince. Now I'll never see my daddy again. And you may never see your friend again."

They heard a voice. But it was just Stu. "I'll go turn on the sprinkler, Deed!" the babies heard him say as he stepped outside.

Then suddenly they all heard something else.

TUM-TA-DA-TUMMMMMM! A trumpet fanfare sounded.

"They're here!" Max squeaked quietly to the others.

"The bell worked!" Tommy said happily.

"His Royal Majesty, the king, and his Royal Majesty, Prince Maximilian!" Perkins the butler announced.

Someone ran straight into the backyard, followed closely by Perkins, who was red-faced and breathless. It was Chuckie. The other babies gave a squeal of delight.

Stu stood holding the sprinkler and gawking as the king stepped out into the backyard too. The sprinkler had begun spraying, but Stu didn't seem to notice that he was getting wet. Didi, Chas, Howard, and Betty, all openmouthed with astonishment, followed the king into the yard.

"Please pardon the intrusion, sir," the king said to Stu. "I recall meeting you at the party, and wanted to have a look at your workshop."

"Uh, sure, no problem, Your Highness!" Stu said, hastily setting the sprinkler down. "It's down in the basement, right this way." Squelching a bit with each step he took, Stu escorted the king past the other adults and toward the basement. The rest of the grown-ups, including Perkins, followed them quietly back into the house like stunned sheep. Grandpa Lou stirred briefly beneath his newspaper, then fell back to sleep.

When the grown-ups were back inside, Chuckie told the other babies about his own adventures. Max stood nearby, shyly listening.

"Oh, Chuckie!" Tommy said happily. "It sure is good to see you again."

"It would be good to see you, too, Tommy, 'ceptin I can't really see much of anything without my glasses," said Chuckie.

Max whipped the glasses off of his nose and handed them to Chuckie. Chuckie put them on, then peered at Max. "Gee, thanks, Your Majestic," he said.

"Call me Max," Max said, grinning.

Chuckie looked surprised. "Okay, Max."

"Hey!" said Kimi. "Let's play in the sprinkler!"

"What's a sprinkler?" asked Max.

Lil's eyes widened. "You mean you

never played in a sprinkler afore?"

Max shook his head.

"You just run in it and get all wet," Phil explained, pointing toward the sprinkler that Stu had turned on.

Max grinned. "I gotta get one of these when I go back to the palace," he said. The king and the rest of the grown-ups had come back outside. "Uh-oh," said Stu. "Look at the kids! They've taken their clothes off!"

Sure enough, the babies were wearing nothing but their diapers and squealing with delight as they ran through the sprinkler.

"Gee," Chas said, staring at the babies. "If it weren't for Chuckie's glasses, I could swear he looks exactly like the prince. Nah." He shrugged, and chuckled. "Guess we better get those wet kids back home for a bath!"

The king, too, was staring from Max to

Chuckie and back again. Then he smiled to himself and shook his head.

Perkins hurried over to where the babies were frolicking. "This won't do at all, Your Highness!" he said, scooping Max up in his arms. Max turned to Chuckie and grinned. Chuckie grinned right back.

Chas picked up Chuckie and tickled him under the chin. Then he picked up Kimi. "Let's go home and see your mother," he said, giving them each a hug.

Chuckie and Kimi hugged their dad right back.

Chapter 8

"So, I guess you *have* been telling the truth about being so chummy with the king," said Drew. He didn't look very happy about it.

"Yeah, well," Stu said breezily as he polished his fingernails on his sleeve. "He's a nice enough guy, the king. Did I mention he dropped by the house? We got to talking, and we found out we have a lot in common. So then he invited us all to come here to the airport to see them off."

"There they are!" said Angelica, who was sitting up on her father's shoulders.

Trumpets sounded.

Sitting in their strollers, Chuckie, Tommy, Kimi, Phil, and Lil strained to see. Suddenly Chuckie felt a tug on his sleeve. He turned around. It was Max.

"Hi," said Max. "I just got away for a minute 'cause I wanted to say thank you. You were right about my new mommy and my sister. They're really great. My stepmommy's not wicked at all."

Chuckie smiled. "I thought you'd like 'em." He felt a tugging on his other sleeve and turned. It was Isabel.

"I just wanted you to know I think I'm gonna like being a princess. Me and my brother are making changes around here. I told our mom and dad we want to wear comfy clothes from now on."

Max showed Chuckie what he was wearing. It was a T-shirt just like Chuckie's.

"And we're gonna get to play outside as much as we want," he added.

"And we don't have to do boring hissitry lessons till we get older," said Isabel.

"And I got *Blammo-Man* videos to take home with me," Max said, all excited.

"That's great, you guys," said Chuckie.

"I had fun bein' your sister," said Isabel.

"And, I had fun bein' you, Chuckie," said Max. "Remember," he said, addressing all the babies, "if you ever come to my country, I'll make you knightses and ladies. 'Cept that Angelica. She . . ."

Just then Drew took Angelica off his shoulders and set her down on the ground near the babies. She looked from Max to Chuckie and back again. She gulped. "Heh. Heh. So, you mean, you really were tellin' the truth? You . . . you . . . you really are a real prince?"

Max crossed his arms sternly. "Yup," he said.

"Well, I knew that. I was just kiddin' around, just *pretending* to be mean to you. You know that, right, Your Maddesty?"

"No," Max said in the same tone. "But you listen here, Angelica. I command you to start bein' nicer to these babies. Or else *You Know What* could happen."

"Does he mean he'll throw her in his dumb-geon?" Tommy whispered to Chuckie.

"Nah, I don't think he really means it," Chuckie whispered back.

Angelica went a little pale, then curled one hand behind her back and crossed her fingers. "Sure thing. I'll be nice to them from now on. Really I will. Have a nice trip, Your Hightop."

And as Max hurried away with his sister to rejoin their parents, he turned to Chuckie and winked.

About the Author

Sarah Willson has written more than eighty children's books, many of them about the Rugrats! She has been a newspaper cartoonist, and once played semiprofessional basketball. She lives in Connecticut with her husband, three small children, and two large cats.